KID'S CUISINE

BY DOREEN RITCHIE

Editor:
Janet Stewart

Illustrators:
Rick Rowden   Gord Frazer
Renee Mansfield   Tina Seemann

Copyright © 1988 by Hayes Publishing Ltd.

All rights reserved. No part of this book may be reproduced or transmitted in any form or by any means, electronic or mechanical, including photocopying and recording, or by any information storage or retrieval system, without permission in writing from the publisher.

ISBN 0-88625-153-2

3312 Mainway, Burlington, Ontario L7M 1A7, Canada
2045 Niagara Falls Blvd., Unit 14, Niagara Falls, NY 14304, U.S.A.

Printed in Hong Kong

CONTENTS

About This Book.. 3
Our Well-stocked Kitchen..................................... 4

Breakfast
Pancakes, Waffles, French Toast..................... 6
Sour Cream Coffee Cake................................... 8
Fruits, Juices, Cereals... 9
Eggs... 10

Lunch
Hot Diggity Dogs... 12
Juicy Hamburgers... 13
Sloppy Joes.. 14
Chewy Cheese, English Muffins..................... 15
Sandwiches.. 16
Soups... 18
Scrunchy Salads... 22

Main Dishes
Lasagna... 25
Noodle Mania... 27
Meatloaf Madness.. 28
Chomper Chops... 29
Chicken.. 30
Dynamite Veggies... 32
Dips.. 39

Scrumptious Snacks.. 40

Conversion Tables.. 47
Glossary.. 47

ABOUT THIS BOOK

Everyone loves a good meal. This book will help you become a real chef. If you follow our instructions, you'll be a "junior gourmet" in no time at all!

If you're a beginner in the kitchen, get some help from someone with more experience. The recipes with a red light beside them are more difficult than some of the others. Read through the recipe before you begin to make sure you understand it. Then gather up the ingredients and equipment you'll need. Watch carefully for the yellow light. Wherever you see this sign, the method gets a little tricky. If you continue alone, be extra cautious. When you see the green light, read the instructions and then begin. You won't have too much trouble with these recipes.

Most measurements in this book are in imperial measure. If you want to convert to metric, use the conversion table on page 47. And, if you're unsure about equipment or words used in the recipes, check our well-stocked kitchen on the next page, or the glossary on page 47. You'll find what you need there.

3

OUR WELL-STOCKED KITCHEN

1. small bowl
2. medium bowl
3. large bowl
4. slotted spoon
5. spatula
6. grapefruit knife
7. knife
8. sifter
9. double boiler
10. wooden spoon
11. ladle
12. skewer
13. toothpick
14. bamboo steamer
15. pastry blender/masher
16. candy thermometer
17. wok
18. scissors
19. oven mitts
20. strainer
21. blender
22. measuring cup
23. pot
24. large pot
25. round pan
26. lemon squeezer
27. electric mixer
28. colander
29. weigh scale
30. skillet/frying pan
31. hand mixer
32. whisk
33. garlic crusher
34. lifter
35. fondue

BREAKFAST

PANCAKES, WAFFLES AND FRENCH TOAST

Ingredients:
- 1 1/2 cups all-purpose flour
- 2 tablespoons white sugar
- 3 teaspoons baking powder
- 1/2 teaspoon salt.
- 1 egg, beaten
- 1 3/4 cups milk
- 2 tablespoons vegetable oil

Flip, flop, flap! Making flapjacks.

Method:

If you have a sifter, use it to sift dry ingredients together into a large bowl. Otherwise, just put the dry ingredients lightly into the bowl. Make a hole with your finger in the middle of the mixture (make sure your hands are clean!). Stir the liquid ingredients together with a whisk in a small bowl, and pour this into the hole you just made in the dry mixture. Beat with an electric mixer or a wooden spoon until you have a nice, smooth batter.

Heat a frying pan on the stove until drops of cold water dance across the surface. (Or heat an electric frying pan to 380°F). Be careful -- both of these will be very hot! Grease the pan lightly with butter or oil. Using a small measuring cup or a large spoon, pour batter onto the pan to make a pancake just the size you like! Flip the pancake over with a lifter when bubbles appear on the surface of the batter.

Continue making your pancakes until all the batter is gone, or until you're full! Top them with honey butter made by beating equal amounts of butter and honey together until fluffy. If you eat the pancakes as they're cooking, be careful that the oil or butter doesn't get too hot. If the batter begins to thicken, add more milk and stir. Leftover batter will keep in the refrigerator for a couple of days in an airtight container. Just add a little milk and stir. Then you'll be ready to go again.

French Toast, Honey Style

Ingredients:
- 2 eggs
- 1/4 cup milk
- 1/4 cup liquid honey
- 1/4 teaspoon salt
- 6 - 8 slices bread
- butter

Method:
Crack open the eggs into a large bowl and beat them with a whisk. If you've never cracked an egg, get someone who has to demonstrate for you. Or, if you're really brave, try it yourself. Just be careful you don't get eggshells in the bowl.

Add the milk, honey and salt into the bowl and stir until blended together.

Melt a little butter in a frying pan over MEDIUM heat -- just enough to cover the bottom of the pan. Dip the bread slices into the egg mixture so that both sides are covered and place them in the pan. You'll get gooey fingers, but the end result will be worth it! Cook until golden brown. Top with syrup and dig in!

Waffles — *Quit Waffling Around and Get to Work!*

Ingredients:
- 1 1/2 cups all-purpose flour
- 2 tablespoons white sugar
- 3 teaspoons baking powder
- 1/2 teaspoon salt
- 2 eggs, beaten
- 1 1/2 cups milk
- 1/4 cup melted butter or margarine

Method:
Prepare batter as for pancakes with the new liquid ingredients listed above. Heat your waffle iron according to the manufacturer's instructions. Pour the batter into the hot waffle iron.

Bake until the waffle stops steaming. Serve warm with butter, maple syrup and bacon slices.

Variation --
Cheese and Bacon Waffles
Add half a cup of grated cheese into the waffle batter. Pour into the hot waffle iron and lay crisp bacon slices (see page 10 for bacon cooking directions) on top before baking. You'll finish with yummy cheesy bacon waffles.

7

Sour Cream Coffee Cake

🟢 *A Great Breakfast Treat for Mother's Day, Father's Day -- or any day.*

Ingredients:
- 2 cups all-purpose flour
- 1 teaspoon baking powder
- 1 teaspoon baking soda
- 1/2 teaspoon salt
- 1 cup sugar
- 1/2 cup butter
- 2 eggs, beaten
- 1 teaspoon vanilla flavoring
- 1 cup sour cream

Method: Preheat your oven to 375°F.

Sift all dry ingredients into a small bowl and stir them together. Cream the butter in a separate bowl (medium to large size) using an electric mixer or wooden spoon. Add the sugar and beat until creamy. Then add the eggs and vanilla flavoring and continue mixing until smooth.

Alternately add the dry ingredients and the sour cream to the creamed mixture. Add them a spoonful at a time, and mix until blended into a smooth batter. Without an electric mixer you'll need a strong arm!

Spread this mixture into a greased 8-inch square pan.

Topping:

Ingredients:
- 1/2 cup brown sugar
- 1 teaspoon cinnamon
- 1/2 cup chopped walnuts

Method:
Mix the ingredients together. Sprinkle this topping over the cake batter in the pan and bake at 375°F for 35 minutes. Using oven mitts, remove the pan from the oven and serve warm or cool.

Variation:
Add 1/2 cup chocolate chips to the batter. Add 1/2 cup chocolate chips to the topping. You'll have chocolate flavored coffee cake!

FRUITS, JUICES AND CEREALS

Grapefruit --

This tangy breakfast fruit is for all you sourpusses!

Halve the grapefruit, remove as many seeds as you can, and place the fruit in a bowl. Next, separate the fruit sections for easy removal from the grapefruit to your mouth. Use a knife that's fairly sharp, or a grapefruit knife, and cut around the grapefruit just inside the skin. Then criss-cross along the line of each section. If you need some sweetening up, sprinkle a little sugar on top and decorate with red cherries, strawberries or another of your favorite fruits.

Broiled Grapefruit
After separating the fruit sections, sprinkle with brown sugar, and broil until the sugar melts -- about 7 to 8 minutes.

Not Just Another Bowl of Cereal...

Liven up your everyday cereal with your favorite fruit. Or, use a little imagination and drop in marshmallows, chocolate chips, coconut or peanut butter. If you're really adventurous, you might even add pickles! Don't forget the milk!

Mix and Match Fruit and Juice

Blueberries, oranges, bananas and grapes; strawberries, canteloupe – they all taste great! Gather your favorite fruits and cover them with your favorite juice. Think up your own combination, or use orange juice, grapefruit juice or pineapple juice.

9

Egg-in-a-Cup

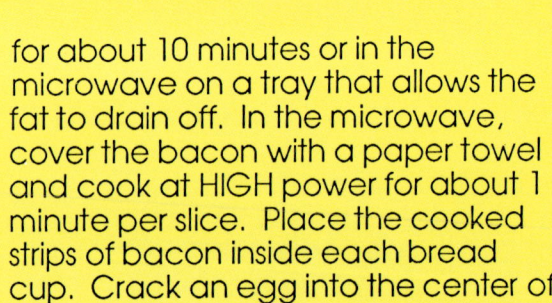

Ingredients:
- bread slice (for each person)
- cooked bacon slice - in microwave or oven
- egg (for each person)
- butter

Method:
Butter the bread and place buttered side down in each of the cups in a muffin pan. Cook a few strips of bacon under the broiler for about 10 minutes or in the microwave on a tray that allows the fat to drain off. In the microwave, cover the bacon with a paper towel and cook at HIGH power for about 1 minute per slice. Place the cooked strips of bacon inside each bread cup. Crack an egg into the center of the bread cup. Make as many cups as you and your friends or family can eat. Bake them in the oven at 350°F for 20 minutes. Remove with oven mitts and enjoy your egg-in-a-cup while it's hot.

Crazy Mixed-up Eggs

Crack two eggs for each person into a bowl. For each egg add 2 tablespoons of milk, and a pinch of salt and/or pepper to taste. Scramble them with a whisk. Add a little butter to a frying pan and melt over MEDIUM heat. The butter should just cover the bottom of the pan.

Tip: A Teflon-coated pan prevents sticking and is easier to clean afterward -- a great plus for any chef!

Pour your scrambled eggs into the buttered pan. Use a spatula to move the mixture gently from the bottom of the pan and mix the eggs around. Be patient! Don't increase the heat. The eggs will soon become fluffy. Continue stirring gently until almost all the liquid has gone. Remove the pan from the heat and serve immediately -- scrambled eggs cool fast!

Variation:
Sprinkle some grated cheese on the eggs while they are in the pan. Or add chopped ham, chopped tomatoes or sliced mushrooms. It's fun to experiment with new taste sensations!

Soft-boiled Eggs

Place eggs still in their shells in a pot and cover them with cold water. Place the pot on the stove and bring the water to a boil using HIGH heat.

Reduce the heat to LOW once the water has boiled and simmer for 3 1/2 minutes.

Remove the eggs from the pot with a slotted spoon and place in an egg cup.

Carefully slice the top of the egg off with a knife and add salt to taste. Cut your bread into finger slices and dip them into the yummy yellow yolk.

Did You Know?

You will get four times as much iron from an egg if you drink orange juice at the same meal.

There is no difference between brown and white eggs -- they have the same nutritional value and flavor.

LUNCH

*Crunch, crunch, I love to munch
A bunch of treats, to eat for lunch!*

Microwave Method:
Place wiener in bun and wrap it in a paper napkin. Cook in the microwave oven at HIGH power for 25 to 35 seconds, or for one minute if the bun and wiener haven't been defrosted. Slap on your favorite toppings (mustard, relish, ketchup, onions, etc.), and cool your thirst with a glass of cold milk!

Hot Diggity Dogs

Crescent Roll Dogs

Use one package of 8 refrigerated crescent rolls. Cut out crescent shapes and wrap them around the wiener. Place them on a cookie sheet and bake in the oven at 375°F for about 10 minutes. For a really special dog, line the dough with half a slice of cheese before wrapping it around the wiener.

Cheese and Bacon Dogs

With a fairly sharp knife, cut down the middle of the wiener to make a slit and fill it with grated cheddar cheese. Stuff in as much as you like. Then wrap a strip of bacon around the wiener and stick a toothpick through it to keep it closed. Broil or bake these dogs until the cheese melts and the wiener begins to brown. Serve them as they are or on a hot dog bun.

Alison's Juicy Hamburgers
(serves 6)

Method:

Mix all the ingredients together and divide the mix into six sections. Roll each section into a ball and flatten it out to form a hamburger patty.

Barbecue or broil the patties for 6 to 8 minutes on each side, brushing with barbecue sauce. Turn the hamburgers only once and don't flatten them out with the lifter; otherwise, the juices will be squeezed out.

Add cheese if you like when the second side is nearly cooked.

Serve on a hamburger bun and pile on all your favorite toppings.

Ingredients:
- 1 pound ground beef
- 1 tablespoon dry flaked onion
- 1/2 cup water or milk
- 1 teaspoon salt
- 1 teaspoon Worcestershire sauce
- 1/4 teaspoon pepper

SLOP WITH SLOPPY JOES

Ingredients:
- 1 pound ground beef
- 1 cup chopped green onions
- 1 cup chopped celery
- pitted olives (optional)
- 1 cup ketchup
- 1 tablespoon brown sugar
- 1 tablespoon white vinegar
- 2 tablespoons prepared mustard
- salt to taste (a pinch will do)

Sloppy Joes

Method:
Break up the beef with a wooden spoon in a large frying pan over MEDIUM heat.

Stir it constantly until brown. Pour the meat into a large sieve, over a bowl, to drain off any excess fat. Leave the fat to harden and when it does, throw it out with the garbage. Return the meat to the pan and add the remaining ingredients.

Mix until blended. Reduce the heat, cover and simmer for 30 minutes. Spoon the cooked mixture over toasted hamburger buns or English muffins.

Have plenty of paper towels on hand while eating your sloppy joes!

NEVER LEAVE A FRYING PAN UNATTENDED, AND TURN OFF THE HEAT IMMEDIATELY AFTER COOKING IS COMPLETED!

HOT OFF THE GRILL...

Chewy Cheese

Ingredients: • bread (two slices per person) • cheese • butter • pickles

Method:
Place cheese (either a processed cheese slice or slices of cheddar) between two slices of bread. Butter the outer sides of the bread. Heat a frying pan over MEDIUM heat. Place the sandwiches on the pan, butter side down, and cook for 2 to 3 minutes until golden brown. Turn the sandwich with a lifter and repeat for the other side. Remove from the pan. Cut into quarters or triangles and serve with crunchy pickles and a glass of milk.

Variations:
Add sliced tomatoes, bacon, ham, or anything else you like, to the inside of the sandwich with the cheese for a really original sandwich.

Other methods:
You can grill your sandwiches under the broiler, or cook them in an electric sandwich grill, using the same preparation noted above.

English Muffins with Seafood and Cheese

Method: Soften the butter in a small bowl with an electric mixer or wooden spoon. Mix in the cheese, seafood and seasonings. Spread the mixture on halved muffins. Place them on a cookie sheet and broil until bubbly.

Ingredients:
- 4 English muffins
- 1/2 cup butter
- 1 cup cheddar cheese, grated
- 1 - 7 ounce can crabmeat or cocktail shrimp, drained
- garlic salt and pepper to taste

SANDWICHES

Did you know that sandwiches were invented and named after an English nobleman, the Earl of Sandwich? He wanted a portable and easily eaten meal that he could take with him. Not to school, however, but to the gambling table!

The basics of sandwich-making are simple: Spread two slices of bread with butter or margarine. Spread one with your favorite filling, and place the other slice on top. Cut the sandwich into squares, triangles, rectangles or circles. Then dig in!

Tips:
The butter or margarine should always be soft for easy spreading. Spread the butter or margarine right to the edges -- this prevents the bread from drying out, and from becoming too soggy when the filling is added.

Serve sandwiches for any meal when you need something fast and good. Carrot and celery sticks will liven up a sandwich meal. If you're having a party or making sandwiches for the rest of your family, arrange a bunch of them on a tray, decorated with parsley, and surprise your family with a ready-made meal. Or pack them in your lunch bag with a few other treats for a great take-away lunch.

16

Some Simple Fillings:

Peanut butter with honey or bananas
Bologna meat and relish
Roast beef and mayonnaise (or mustard)
Ham with cheese and mustard (or mayonnaise)
Sliced tomato and lettuce

Fillings with Pizzazz!

Tuna Salad:
Open a can of tuna, but before removing the lid, press it down and drain off the liquid the tuna is packed in. Be careful -- the edges of the can are sharp! Remove the tuna from the can and put it in a small bowl. Chop half a stalk of celery, and if you like onions, chop the white bulb part of a green onion. Add the celery, onion and a little mayonnaise to the tuna - just enough to bind the ingredients. Add salt and pepper to taste. Mix together and spread onto your choice of bread.

Salmon Salad:
Same method as for tuna, but use salmon instead.

Egg Salad:
Cook and peel the shells from 3 or 4 hard-boiled eggs (see below). Place the eggs in a small bowl and chop them with a pastry blender, or use a fork to mash them. Add celery, onion and mayonnaise as for the tuna, but also add a teaspoon of prepared mustard. Mix it well and spread it on your bread.

Hard-boiled Eggs:
Prepare as for soft-boiled eggs (page 11), but simmer for 10 minutes instead of 3 1/2. Cool the eggs immediately in cold running water - delays cause a dark rim to form around the yolk. Break the shells by giving them a light crack on a hard surface (the counter) or with a spoon. Roll the egg between your hands to further crack the shell. Peel off the shell under running water, starting with the large end.

Tip:
Adding a little salt to the water before boiling hardens the shell and makes it easier to peel the egg.

Hard-boiled eggs are not only used as a base for egg salad. They can be used: unsliced as part of your lunch or picnic; sliced as a sandwich filling; or sliced as a garnish or ingredient in other salads.

RAINY DAY SUNSHINE

IN A CUP OR A BOWL, CANNED AND HOMEMADE SOUPS ARE THE BEST WAY TO GO FOR A WARM FILLING LUNCH!

Canned Soup with a Difference

Canned soups are great when you're in a rush! Why not try something different by mixing two varieties? The following are all condensed soups. Adding milk instead of water gives a creamier taste. Mix the two soups well. Heat with gentle stirring until almost boiling, but do not boil.

Varieties:

Chicken-Pea Parsley Soup

- 1 can green pea soup
- 1 can cream of chicken soup
- 1 can milk
- 1 can water

Sprinkle a bit of parsley on top

Really Chickeny Star Soup

- 1 can chicken noodle soup
- 1 can chicken with stars soup
- 2 cans water

Tomato-Beef Soup

- 1 can tomato soup
- 1 can beef noodle soup
- 2 cans water

Chicken-Veggie Soup

- 1 can chicken gumbo soup
- 1 can vegetable soup
- 2 cans water

Chicken-Mushroom Soup

- 1 can cream of chicken soup
- 1 can cream of mushroom soup
- 2 cans milk

Ingredients:
- 1 large onion, sliced
- 4 tablespoons butter
- 1 can tomato soup
- 1 (soup) can milk
- 1/4 teaspoon Worcestershire sauce
- 1 1/2 cups cheddar cheese

Cheesy Tomato Soup

Method:

1. Melt butter in a large saucepan over MEDIUM heat.

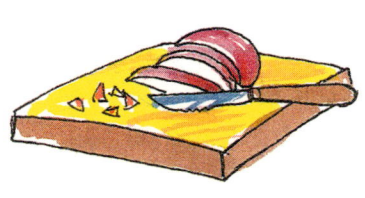

2. Carefully slice the onion in thin slices, with a fairly sharp knife. Add the butter. Saute, or simmer together, until soft.

3. Add the tomato soup, stirring constantly. Slowly pour in the milk, stirring gently with a wooden spoon.

4. Bring to a boil. Add the Worcestershire sauce.

5. Reduce the heat to LOW and slowly add grated cheese, stirring until all the cheese has completely melted.

Ladle into soup bowls and serve with toasted English muffins, hamburger buns, crackers or toast.

That Good Homemade Flavor!

Ingredients:
- 1 - 28 ounce can of tomatoes
- 1 small onion, chopped
- 1 tablespoon butter
- 3 tablespoons flour
- 2 cups milk
- salt and pepper to taste

Cream of Tomato Soup

Method:

Melt butter in a large saucepan over MEDIUM heat. Add onions and saute for 2 to 3 minutes.

Stirring constantly with a wooden spoon, add flour and cook for 1 to 2 minutes. Add tomatoes.

Increase the heat to HIGH and bring to a boil, stirring all the time. Reduce the heat to MEDIUM and slowly pour in milk.

Season with salt and pepper. Let soup simmer about 20-30 minutes. Remove from heat.

DO NOT BOIL -- TURN OFF HEAT!

Ladle into soup bowls and serve with crackers, sandwiches or salad.

Optional - If you like a creamier soup, mix the soup in a blender or with a hand mixer.

The Gourmet's Touch...

Ingredients:
- 2 large onions, sliced
- 1/4 cup butter or margarine
- 1 can consomme or beef broth
- 1 can water
- 1 tablespoon Worcestershire sauce
- grated mozzarella cheese
- grated Parmesan cheese
- sugar, salt, pepper - a pinch to taste
- 4 slices of toasted French bread

Easy French Onion Soup

This is really an easy soup to make. It can be satisfying for lunch, accompanied by a salad, or used to start off an evening meal.

Method:

Melt the butter or margarine in a large saucepan. Add onions and saute for 3 to 4 minutes until light brown. Add the consomme, water and Worcestershire sauce, and bring to a boil.

Turn the heat down slightly and simmer for 45 minutes.

Add salt, pepper and a pinch of sugar to taste. Pour into four individual ovenproof bowls with a soup ladle until the bowls are 1/2 to 3/4 full.

Place a slice of toasted French bread on top of the soup in the bowl. Sprinkle with mozzarella and Parmesan cheese.

Put the bowls on a strong baking sheet and broil until the cheese begins to bubble.

Remove with oven mitts and serve while hot.

SCRUNCHY SALADS

Salads are made with vegetables and fruit. They can be simple or complicated, crisp or gooey! Use a salad as the main course for your lunch or to accompany other foods at lunch or dinner.

A Caesar Salad Success!

Ingredients:
- 1 cup Caesar salad-flavored croutons
- 1 cup Caesar salad dressing
- 1/4 cup Parmesan cheese (optional)
- bacon bits
- 1 medium head Romaine lettuce

Method:
Wash and dry the lettuce. Tear into bite-size pieces and put in a large salad bowl. Add the croutons and salad dressing. Toss well and sprinkle with bacon bits and Parmesan cheese. Serve immediately.

Mandarin Spinach Delight

Ingredients:
- 1 bag fresh spinach, stems removed
- 1 can mandarin oranges, drained
- 2 - 3 green onions, chopped
- 6 - 8 raw mushrooms, sliced
- 1 cup Herb & Garlic dressing

Method:
Wash and drain spinach. Place in a large bowl. Add other ingredients except dressing and toss with salad servers. Chill until you serve with the cup of salad dressing.

Toss It Up!

Ingredients:
- 1 head iceberg lettuce, washed and dried with paper towels
- 2 - 3 green onions, chopped
- 2 stalks celery, sliced
- 1 small cucumber, sliced
- 1 large tomato, sliced
- salad dressing of your choice

Method:

Be careful when slicing the tomatoes, cucumbers and celery -- you might cut yourself instead of the food! Tear the lettuce into bite-size pieces and place in a glass or wooden salad bowl.

Add the remaining ingredients and toss lightly with salad servers or two wooden spoons.

Hatching Shapes Salad

Ingredients:
- 6 - 10 large lettuce leaves, washed and dried
- 1 hard-boiled egg per person (see page 17)
- mayonnaise
- parsley

Method:

Cover the plate with crisp lettuce leaves. Slice the eggs thinly. You can use an egg slicer gadget that has thin wires to cleanly cut through the egg, or a knife to make thin slices. Arrange the egg slices in fun patterns on top of the lettuce.

Top with a spoonful of mayonnaise and garnish with parsley.

Honey Cream Fruit Salad

Method:
Mix the dressing ingredients in a medium bowl until blended. Chill in the refrigerator.

Wash the fruit and cut into bite-size pieces.

Place the lettuce leaves on a plate and cover them with fruit pieces. Top with honey cream dressing and serve.

Tips:
Dip apple and pear slices in lemon juice to prevent browning. Scoop out small balls from the melons and canteloupes with a spoon.

Ingredients:
- 6 - 10 large lettuce leaves, washed and dried
- a mixture of your favorite fruits

Dressing Ingredients:
- 1 cup sour cream or plain yogurt
- 2 teaspoons honey
- 1 teaspoon lemon juice

Easy Waldorf Salad

Ingredients:
- 1 cup diced apples
- 1 cup seedless grapes, halved
- 1 cup diced celery
- 1/2 cup walnut pieces (optional)
- 2 tablespoons lemon juice
- 1/2 cup mayonnaise

Method:
Throw the celery, fruits, and nuts into a bowl. If you have a fancy glass bowl, use it. Mix the mayonnaise and lemon juice together and add to the fruit. Toss lightly with serving spoons. Chill in the refrigerator for about 1/2 hour and serve.

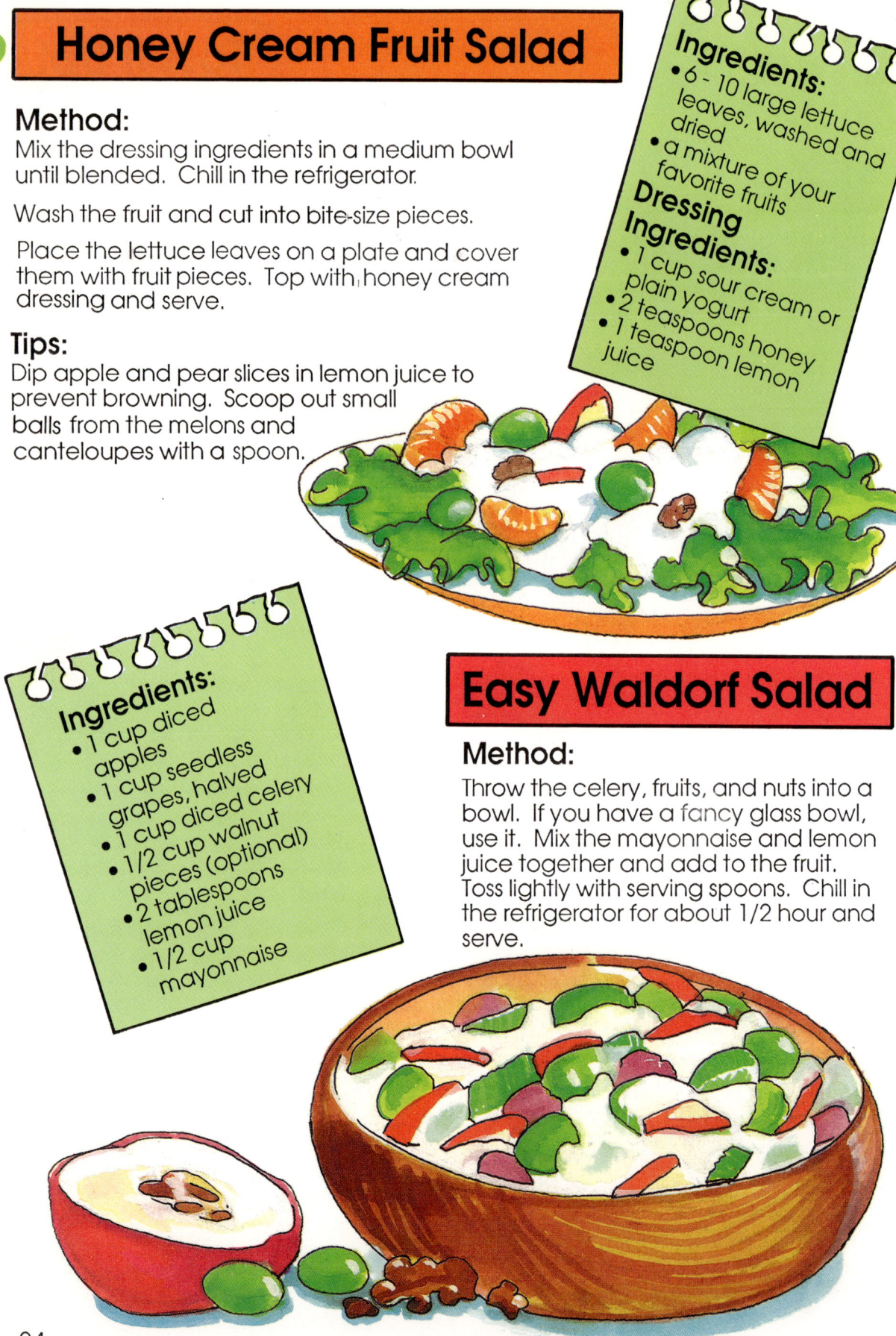

MAIN DISHES

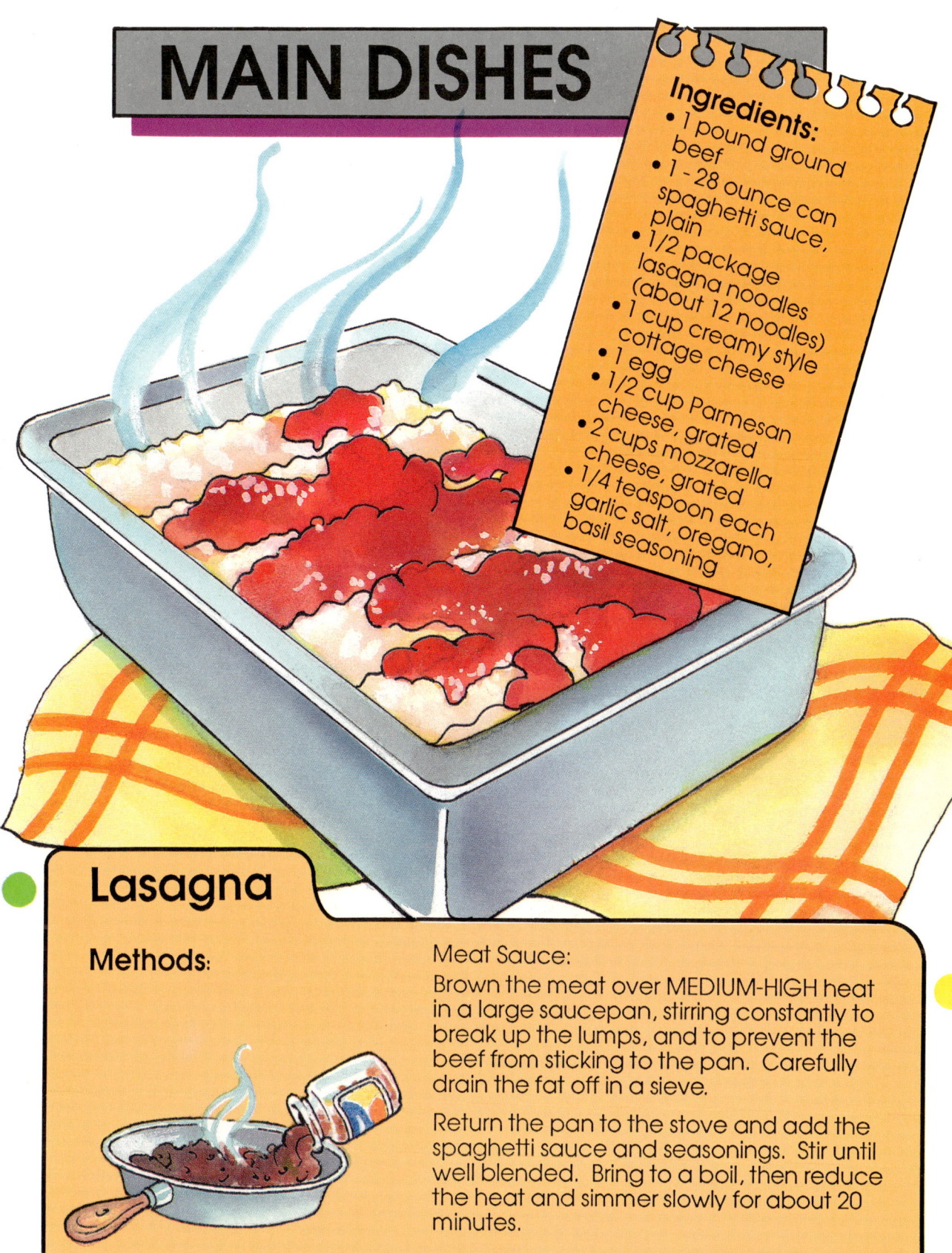

Ingredients:
- 1 pound ground beef
- 1 - 28 ounce can spaghetti sauce, plain
- 1/2 package lasagna noodles (about 12 noodles)
- 1 cup creamy style cottage cheese
- 1 egg
- 1/2 cup Parmesan cheese, grated
- 2 cups mozzarella cheese, grated
- 1/4 teaspoon each garlic salt, oregano, basil seasoning

Lasagna

Methods:

Meat Sauce:

Brown the meat over MEDIUM-HIGH heat in a large saucepan, stirring constantly to break up the lumps, and to prevent the beef from sticking to the pan. Carefully drain the fat off in a sieve.

Return the pan to the stove and add the spaghetti sauce and seasonings. Stir until well blended. Bring to a boil, then reduce the heat and simmer slowly for about 20 minutes.

PASTA PERFECT

Noodles:
Cook the noodles separately from the meat sauce in a large pot. Follow the instructions on the package. After they're cooked, drain, and rinse the noodles under cold water.

Cream Sauce:
Mix the cottage cheese, egg and Parmesan cheese together in a small bowl.

Now for the fun part! Assemble the following layers in order in a large casserole dish, or a 9x13-inch pan. Make sure the layers completely cover the whole dish.

Layers:

First spread a thin layer of sauce on the bottom of the dish. Then, assemble:

    1/2 of the noodles
    1/3 of the meat sauce
    1/2 of the cream sauce
    1/2 of the grated mozzarella cheese

Repeat the first three layers a second time. Add the remaining noodles. Then top with the remaining 1/3 meat sauce, and sprinkle the remaining 1/2 mozzarella cheese. Sprinkle with Parmesan cheese. Bake in the oven at 375°F for 50 - 60 minutes. Remove from the oven, and let stand in the pan for 10 minutes before serving. Serve with your Easy Caesar Salad and fresh, crusty buns.

Another great reason for cooking lasagna:
It's even better the next day, heated up for lunch!

NOODLE MANIA

Ingredients:
- 1 1/2 pounds ground beef
- 1 envelope packaged spaghetti sauce mix (if you can't get this, use 1/2 teaspoon each of basil, oregano and rosemary mixed together with a pinch of pepper)
- 1 small can tomato paste
- 1 can mushroom pieces and juice
- 1 - 19 ounce can tomatoes
- 1 medium onion, sliced
- 1/4 teaspoon garlic salt
- salt and pepper to taste
- 1/2 package spaghetti

Spaghetti and Meat Sauce

Method:
Brown the ground beef in a large saucepan, stirring occasionally to break it up. Drain off the excess fat in a sieve over a bowl. Let the fat harden and then throw it out with the garbage. Return the meat to the pan. Add all the other ingredients except the spaghetti and stir well. Slowly bring to a boil, then lower the heat, and simmer the sauce for 1 1/4 hours. Stir occasionally over the time period.

While this is simmering, cook the spaghetti according to package directions. Do not overcook the spaghetti. Drain the spaghetti when cooked and then rinse under cold water for a second to remove the starch. Put the spaghetti in a bowl, or back into the pot, and add a bit of butter. This will make it creamier. Then arrange the spaghetti on a large platter, and spoon the meat sauce on top. Add a sprig of parsley, and serve with your favorite salad and crusty bread. Umm...delicious!

Meatloaf Madness

Ingredients:
- 1 can condensed tomato soup
- 1 1/2 pounds ground beef
- 1/2 cup fine bread crumbs or rolled oats
- 1 egg
- 1/3 cup finely sliced onions
- salt and pepper to taste
- 1 teaspoon horseradish (optional)

Method:
Preheat the oven to 350°F. Combine the beef, bread crumbs, onions, salt and pepper in a large bowl. You might want to use your hands to mix this. It's pretty gooey but mixes well. Make sure your hands are clean.

Mix together with a fork. Add the egg and 1/2 the can of soup, and mix again until blended. Spread the mixture in a shallow baking pan, which you've already greased, buttered or sprayed with oil.

Place on the middle shelf of the oven and bake for 40 minutes.

Wearing oven mitts, remove the meatloaf from the oven, and top with the remaining 1/2 can of soup (add the horseradish to this if desired). Return to the oven and bake for 5 more minutes.

Serve with baked potatoes, vegetables, salad, or just as a meatloaf sandwich.

Chomper Chops

EASY AND TASTY, PORK AT ITS BEST

Method:

Heat the oven to 375°F. Place the chops in a single layer in a greased baking pan. Cover over with foil and bake for 20 minutes. Using oven mitts, remove the chops from the oven and drain off the excess fat.

Pour mushroom soup over the chops, adding a little water to the sauce if desired. Bake uncovered for 20-30 minutes longer, or until tender.

Serve with potatoes and vegetables.

Ingredients:
- large pork chops
- 1 can condensed mushroom soup
- salt and pepper to taste

A CHICKEN IN THE OVEN

Ingredients:
- 4 large chicken breasts
- 1 can condensed mushroom soup
- 1 can whole mushrooms with liquid
- 1 cup sour cream
- paprika

Dreamy, Creamy Chicken

Method:

Preheat the oven to 350°F. Wash the chicken breasts and pat dry with a paper towel. If you don't like the chicken skin, pull it off now.

Place the breasts in a large shallow casserole dish. Combine the soup, mushrooms with liquid, and sour cream in a small bowl and mix well with a wooden spoon. Pour over the chicken and sprinkle with paprika.

Bake uncovered chicken for 1 1/4 hours, until tender.

Serve with vegetables of your choice for a mouthwatering meal.

Ingredients:

- 4 large chicken breasts
- 1/2 cup mayonnaise (optional)
- 1 cup cornflakes
- 1/2 cup butter or margarine
- salt, pepper and paprika to taste

Crunchy Coated Chicken

Method:

Preheat the oven to 350°F. Rinse the chicken under cold water and pat dry with a paper towel. Melt the butter or margarine in a shallow roasting pan or casserole dish in the oven. This will only take a minute or so.

Meanwhile, brush the chicken with mayonnaise if desired, and sprinkle with cornflakes. Season with a pinch of salt, pepper and paprika.

Place the chicken in a casserole dish and bake on the middle shelf of the oven for 1 hour.

Serve this with scalloped potatoes and green vegetables for a meal you'll want to try again and again!

DYNAMITE VEGGIES

Carrots, potatoes, broccoli and peas. Cauliflower, corn and little green beans. Scrumptious veggies for you to eat.

PREPARING VEGGIES

There are many different kinds of vegetables and many ways of preparing them. You can boil, bake, casserole, stir-fry, steam, or eat them raw. The microwave oven is a great way to prepare vegetables fast!

Boiled

Boiling is one of the more traditional methods of cooking vegetables. First wash the vegetables in cold water, scrubbing with a brush if necessary (if they're really dirty). Then follow the steps below to finish preparing the vegetables.

Potatoes: Peel, brush, or leave the skins on. Cook whole or cut in half (30 minutes for whole, 20 for halves).

Carrots: Cut bottoms and tops. Cook whole, sliced into strips or diced (15 minutes for whole, 12 for halves, 10 for diced).

Brussel sprouts
Cut off the bottoms and peel off the outer leaves. Cook whole (15 minutes).

Broccoli: Cook broken into individual flowers (15 minutes).

Cauliflower
Cook whole or broken into individual flowers (25 minutes for whole, about 18 for flowers).

Peas:
Frozen peas should be cooked as they are (4 - 5 minutes). Canned peas - just warm through on low heat.

Corn:
Rip or tear the stalks off. Leave the hub on, if you like, for a handle while you eat the corn, or remove it carefully. Cook whole (approximately 8 - 10 minutes).

Green beans:
Cook whole or cut into bite-size pieces (8 - 10 minutes).

Approximate cooking times are listed, but you may like your vegetables crunchier or softier. Cook them a little longer or shorter, depending on your tastes.

COOKING VEGGIES

Boiled Method:

Place the vegetables in a pot with just enough water to cover and a little salt to taste.

Note: You don't have to cover the whole cauliflower or broccoli. Steam from an inch or two of water will cook the uncovered parts.

Bring the water to a boil, then cover immediately and lower heat. Simmer for the times indicated in the Preparing Veggies Section, or to your taste requirements. The actual cooking time will vary depending on the size of the vegetable pieces. Check by piercing with a thin sharp knife, a fork or skewer. When it goes in easily without having to push, the vegetables are cooked.

The Ultimate Taste Test!

Spoon out a piece of veggie and once it has cooled slightly, taste it. If it's done to your satisfaction, remove the rest from the stove and strain off the water. Add a bit of butter if you like, and serve.

STEAMING VEGGIES

Place the vegetables in a steamer - bamboo or metal. Place the steamer over a pot on the stove that has boiling water in it (an inch or two of water). Turn the heat to MEDIUM and let the vegetables steam over the water for the required cooking time (average 8 - 10 minutes). The vegetables shouldn't be touching the water. This method uses moisture in the form of steam to cook the vegetables tenderly. They are ready when the tests above are successfully completed.

MICROWAVED VEGGIES

Microwaves cook by heating the water that is naturally present in most foods. Most vegetables have high water contents and cook quickly in the microwave oven.

Baked Potatoes

Select 4 medium-sized baking potatoes. Wash and dry well. Prick the skin in a few places with a fork to allow the steam within the potato to escape.

Arrange the potatoes in a circle on a white paper towel in the microwave oven. Microwave at HIGH for about 8 - 10 minutes, turning the potatoes over when halfway through.

Remove the potatoes, test with a skewer or sharp knife, and wrap in a tea towel for 5 minutes.

Cut open the top of the potatoes and add a little butter or sour cream. So tasty!

Carrot Coins

Select 6 medium-sized carrots. Peel off or scrub the skin with a peeler under cold running water, and cut off the tops and bottoms. Slice across the carrots to make coin shapes 1/2" thick, or leave them whole. Place in a medium-size casserole and add 2 tablespoons of water. Cover with a lid. Microwave at HIGH for 8 - 10 minutes, stirring when halfway through.

Remove and let stand covered for 2 minutes. Serve in a casserole dish with a pat of butter.

Cauliflower

Wash and break into flowerettes (bite-sized cauliflower pieces). Proceed as for the carrots, heating for 8 minutes at HIGH, and stirring when halfway through.

Scalloped Potatoes
(In Microwave)

Ingredients:
- 6 medium-sized potatoes, peeled and thinly sliced
- 1/4 cup butter or margarine
- 1 tablespoon dried onion flakes
- 1 teaspoon salt
- 1/4 teaspoon pepper
- 1/4 cup flour
- 2 cups milk

Method:

Combine the butter, onion flakes, salt and pepper in a large glass measuring cup. Microwave at HIGH for 1 to 1 1/2 minutes or until the butter is melted.

Remove from the microwave and stir in the flour a spoonful at a time.

Add the milk and stir until smooth.

Microwave at MEDIUM for 6 - 7 minutes, until the sauce is fairly smooth.

Stir twice during cooking. Put a layer of potatoes in a 2-quart casserole and top with the sauce. Add more layers and top each with sauce. Cover the casserole and microwave at MEDIUM for 25 to 30 minutes or until the potatoes are tender.

Let stand covered for 5 minutes before serving.

Scalloped Potatoes

Ingredients:
- 6 medium potatoes, peeled and thinly sliced
- 1 large onion, sliced
- 3 tablespoons flour
- salt and pepper to taste
- 4 tablespoons butter
- milk
- grated cheese (optional)

Method:

Preheat oven to 350°F. Put a layer of potatoes in a buttered casserole, cover with a layer of onions. Sprinkle with flour to which salt and pepper have been added. Dot with small pieces of butter. Add more layers as above, but finish with a layer of potatoes and butter. Pour in milk until it is seen through the top layer of potatoes. Cover with foil and bake for 1 1/4 hours or until tender.

Note: Remove cover during last 15 minutes of baking to brown the top.

STIR-FRIED VEGETABLES

Preparing vegetables for a stir-fry takes a little time and effort, but this is a fun way of cooking vegetables. Use your imagination -- vary the selection of vegetables from the wide choice available in stores and markets.

CAUTION Don't work with large quantities. It's easier to stir-fry smaller amounts. Set some aside for reheating, if necessary.

Ingredients: The first five ingredients can vary with your likes and dislikes!

- 1/2 cup carrots, sliced
- 1/2 cup celery, sliced
- 1/2 medium onion, sliced
- 1 cup broccoli pieces
- 1/2 cup mushrooms, sliced
- 2 tablespoons water
- 2 tablespoons salad oil
- 1/2 teaspoon salt
- 1/4 teaspoon sugar

Method:

Wash the vegetables and slice or chop them as required. Rinse them in cold water. Add oil to a large dutch oven, frying pan or wok. Use HIGH heat until a piece of vegetable sizzles when added to the oil. Don't let the oil get too hot! Quickly add all the vegetables except the mushrooms, and cook for 5 minutes, stirring quickly and often. Add the remaining ingredients (water, salt, sugar), cover, and cook for another 5 minutes or until the vegetables are tender and crisp. Stir occasionally and add more water, if needed. Serve steaming hot.

For a Chinese flavor, mix the following ingredients in a small measuring cup and add to the vegetables in the pan.

- 1/4 cup chicken broth
- 1 tablespoon honey
- 1 tablespoon vinegar
- 1 tablespoon soya sauce
- 1 1/2 teaspoons cornstarch

Try different combinations:

Cauliflower, zucchini, cucumber, snow peas, green beans, asparagus, water chestnuts, bamboo shoots.

CAUTION Never leave a stir-fry UNATTENDED!

DIP A DEE DO DA...

Doreen's Quick Dip

Ingredients:

- 1/2 cup sour cream
- 1/2 cup plain yogurt or mayonnaise
- 1 package of dry salad dressing mix

Method:

Mix all ingredients together in a small bowl. Spoon into a serving dish and refrigerate for a few hours. Serve with your favorite fresh veggies -- carrot and celery sticks, broccoli, cauliflower, mushrooms, cucumbers, and start dipping!

Spinach Dip

Ingredients:

- 1 package frozen chopped spinach
- 1 cup mayonnaise
- 1 cup sour cream
- 1 package dried vegetable soup
- 1/2 teaspoon lemon juice
- 1 round Russian rye loaf

Method:

Mix all ingredients, except the bread, together in a bowl and refrigerate. Cut the top of the bread with a fairly sharp knife, and cut around the inside about an inch from the crust. Scoop out the bread from the center of the loaf and cut into cubes. Fill the loaf hole with your chilled spinach dip and place on a serving plate, surrounded by the bread cubes for dipping.

SCRUMPTIOUS SNACKS AND DESSERTS

Ingredients:

- 1 - 3 ounce package raspberry jelly powder
- 1 cup boiling water
- 1/2 cup cold water
- 1 cup vanilla ice cream
- 1 cup diced fruit, fresh or canned

Rippling Raspberry Ice Cream Parfait

Method:

Add the jelly powder to an 8-inch square metal pan and pour in the boiling water. Stir until the crystals are completely dissolved. Take half a cup of the jelly liquid from this pan and pour it into a small bowl. Add vanilla ice cream and stir with a wooden spoon until smooth. Spoon this ice cream mixture into 4 parfait glasses until half full. Set aside and chill in refrigerator.

Add half a cup of cold water to the remaining jelly liquid in the square pan and stir until mixed. Place in the freezer until only slightly thickened (about 15 minutes). Add the fruit to the slightly thickened jelly liquid and spoon on top of the ice cream in the parfait glasses. Chill for about 30 minutes before serving.

Variations:

Use orange jelly powder and mandarin oranges. Or use lemon jelly powder and fruit cocktail. Let your imagination take over!

Cherry Cheese Delight

Ingredients:

- 2 cups Graham cracker crumbs
- 4 tablespoons white sugar
- 1/2 cup melted butter
- 2 - 2 ounce packages of whipped topping mix (i.e. Dream Whip)
- 1 - 8 ounce package of cream cheese
- 1 1/2 cups icing sugar
- 2 cans cherry pie filling

Method:

In a large bowl, mix together the crumbs, white sugar and melted butter to form a crumb base. Spread this base over the bottom of a greased 9x13-inch pan. Press down firmly and cool in the refrigerator. Prepare the whipped topping mix according to package directions.

Cheese mixture:

Prepare in a large bowl. Beat the cream cheese until soft with an electric mixer or use a wooden spoon. Gently add the icing sugar until the mixture is smooth and creamy. Add the prepared whipped topping and gently blend together with the wooden spoon. Spread this cheese mixture over the crumb base.

Top with the cherry pie filling, or blend it throughout the cheese mixture to form cherry swirls. Chill before serving. When ready to serve this delicious dessert, cut it in square pieces.

Variations:
Use blueberry or peach pie fillings instead of cherry. Use a 9-inch dish instead of the pan and cut in wedges like a pie. One can of pie filling will be enough topping.

Marvelous Muffins

Ingredients:
- 1 1/2 cups all-purpose flour
- 1/2 cup white sugar
- 3 teaspoons baking powder
- 1/4 teaspoon salt
- 1 cup milk
- 1/3 cup melted butter
- 1 egg
- 1 cup chocolate chips

Chocolate Chip Muffins

Method:

Preheat the oven to 375°F. In a large bowl, sift the flour, baking powder, salt and sugar. If you don't have a sifter, lightly blend the ingredients together with a whisk. Add the chocolate chips and stir with a wooden spoon.

In a small bowl, combine the egg, milk and melted butter and beat them with a whisk. Pour this into the flour mixture, and gently stir together with a wooden spoon. Stir to blend. Don't overmix -- batter should be lumpy!

Grease muffin pans and dust with a little flour, or use paper baking cups in the muffin tin.

Bake in the middle of the oven for 20 minutes.

To check if the muffins are baked, put an oven mitt on and gently pull the tray out a bit. Stick a toothpick into the center of a muffin in the middle of the pan. If it's clean when it's pulled out, your muffins are done!

Blueberry Muffins

Ingredients:
- 1/2 cup white sugar
- 1/4 cup butter or shortening
- 1 egg
- 1 1/2 cups all-purpose flour
- 1/2 teaspoon salt
- 2 teaspoons baking powder
- 1/2 cup milk
- 1 cup blueberries (fresh or frozen)

Method:

Preheat the oven to 375°F. Cream the butter and sugar together with an electric mixer or a wooden spoon for 1 - 2 minutes.

Crack an egg and beat it into the mixture until smooth.

Sift the dry ingredients together in a bowl and stir thoroughly with the wooden spoon. Slowly add the flour alternately with the milk. Stir well with a wooden spoon until just blended.

Gently add in the blueberries, but DO NOT STIR THEM UP!

Grease the muffin cups, or use the paper baking cups in the tins, and fill them 3/4 full with the muffin mixture.

Bake for 20 minutes.

Remove with oven mitts and let cool slightly before eating.

Chocolate Cake

Method:

Preheat the oven to 325°F. Sift the dry ingredients together in a medium-sized bowl. Mix the liquid ingredients together in a large bowl. Slowly add the dry mixture to the liquid ingredients, using an electric mixer on slow speed. Use a spatula to scrape down the sides of the bowl.

Then beat well for about a minute until the batter is smooth. Pour into a greased square pan and smooth evenly with a spatula.

Bake in the middle of the oven for 45 minutes. Remove from the oven and cool in the pan for 10 minutes.

Remove the cake to a wire rack and leave at room temperature until cool. Top this masterpiece with your favorite chocolate icing.

Ingredients:
- 2 cups all-purpose flour
- 1 cup white sugar
- 1/2 teaspoon salt
- 1 1/2 teaspoons baking powder
- 1 1/2 teaspoons baking soda
- 4 tablespoons cocoa
- 1 cup mayonnaise
- 1 cup cold water
- 1 teaspoon vanilla flavoring

Milk Chocolate Icing

Ingredients:
- 2 squares semi-sweet chocolate
- 3 tablespoons soft butter
- 1/2 teaspoon vanilla flavoring
- 2 cups icing sugar
- pinch of salt
- 1/4 cup milk

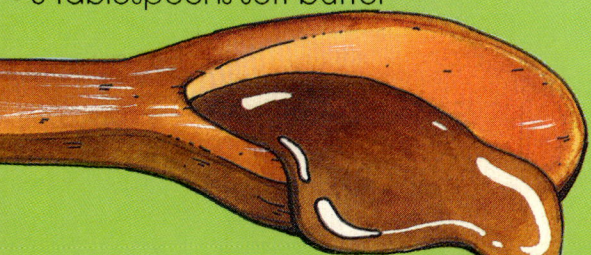

Method:

This icing should only be made when you're ready to use it. That means your cake should be cooled to room temperature.

Cream the butter in a small bowl. Add a little sugar and milk and mix well. Repeat until you use up all the sugar and milk, then add the salt and vanilla. Melt the chocolate in a double boiler. Pour it into the bowl with the other ingredients and mix until blended and smooth. Spread immediately.

Chocolate Chip Cookies

Ingredients:

- 1/2 cup shortening
- 1/2 cup white sugar
- 1/4 cup brown sugar
- 1 egg
- 1 teaspoon vanilla flavoring
- 1 cup sifted all-purpose flour
- 1/2 teaspoon baking soda
- 3/4 teaspoon salt
- 1 cup semi-sweet chocolate chips
- 1/2 cup chopped walnuts (optional)

Method:

Preheat the oven to 375°F. Cream the shortening and sugars in a large mixing bowl with an electric mixer or wooden spoon. Add the egg and vanilla and continue mixing until light and fluffy. If you have to use a wooden spoon, you'll need a lot of arm strength!

Sift together the flour, soda and salt in a small bowl. Slowly add these dry ingredients to the creamed mixture, using the electric mixer at slow speed, or your wooden spoon, until well blended. Stir in the chocolate chips and nuts that you haven't already eaten.

Now for the fun part: Drop teaspoons of the mixture onto a greased cookie sheet about 2 inches apart. Don't eat the dough - you'll get a tummy ache!

Bake in the oven for 10 - 12 minutes and cool on a wire rack. These cookies are great warm with a big glass of milk!

Ingredients:

- 1 can apple pie filling
- 1/3 cup packed brown sugar
- 3/4 cup all-purpose flour
- 1/8 teaspoon cinnamon
- 1/3 cup butter or margarine

Apple Crisp a la Mode

Method:

Preheat the oven to 350°F. Place the apples in an ungreased 9 inch pie plate.

Now the fun begins. Measure the dry ingredients in a medium-size bowl. Add the butter or margarine, and rub the butter into the flour with your fingertips. Keep lifting your hands high above the bowl. Messy but fun, this lets air into the mixture and makes it light and fluffy. Continue with this until you have an even, crumbly mixture. Sprinkle crumbs wildly over the apples and bake for 40-45 minutes. Serve warm with ice cream on top. This tasty treat will melt in your mouth.

Variation:
Try a can of cherry, blueberry or peach pie filling. Be creative with this scrumptious dessert.

Metric Conversions

Measurements in this book are given in imperial measure. Temperatures are in degrees Fahrenheit. Baking pan measurements are given in inches. If you require the metric measurements, this conversion table can be used to make the conversions.

Teaspoons (tsp.) / Tablespoons (tbsp.)
- 1/4 tsp. .... 1 mL
- 1/2 tsp. .... 2 mL
- 1 tsp. .... 5 mL
- 2 tsps. .... 10 mL
- 1 tbsp. .... 15 mL

Cups
- 1/4 cup .... 50 mL
- 1/3 cup .... 75 mL
- 1/2 cup .... 125 mL
- 2/3 cup .... 150 mL
- 3/4 cup .... 175 mL
- 1 cup .... 250 mL

Ounces - Weight
- 1 oz. .... 30 grams
- 2 oz. .... 55 grams
- 3 oz. .... 85 grams
- 4 oz. ...... 125 grams
- 5 oz. ...... 140 grams
- 6 oz. ...... 170 grams
- 7 oz. ...... 200 grams
- 8 oz. ...... 250 grams
- 16 oz. .... 500 grams
- 32 oz. .. 1000 grams

Oven Temperatures Degrees
Fahrenheit   Celcius
- 275 135
- 300 150
- 325 163
- 350 177
- 375 190
- 400 205
- 425 218
- 450 233

Pans
- 8 x 8 inches .... 20 x 20 cm
- 9 x 9 inches .... 22 x 22 cm
- 9 x 13 inches .... 22 x 33 cm

GLOSSARY

Alternately
Add portions of different ingredients, one after the other.

Bake
Cook in the oven.

Batter
Flour mixture too thin to use with hands.

Beat
Mix well with an electric mixer, whisk or wooden spoon.

Boil
Cook food in liquid on HIGH heat with bubbles rising continuously, breaking at the surface.

Broil
Cook by exposing food to direct heat under the broiler in the oven.

Brown
Cook in pan until brown. Either on stove top at MEDIUM to HIGH heat or in a very hot oven.

Chop
Cut food into small pieces with a fairly sharp knife.

Cold Water Dance
Put a few drops of cold water on a hot frying pan. They will bounce about.

Cream
Mix together or beat with a wooden spoon or electric mixer until light and fluffy or soft and smooth.

Crumb
Coat food with crumbs before cooking.

Dash/Pinch
Add less than 1/4 teaspoon.

Dry Ingredients
Solid ingredients such as flour, sugar, and baking powder.

Egg Slicer
A special metal gadget with several thin wires used to slice eggs very thinly.

Fold in
With a gentle up-and-over movement, combine ingredients into a creamed mixture using a wooden spoon or rubber spatula.

Frost
Cover with frosting or icing.

Fry
Cook in fat or oil in an uncovered pan.

Garnish
Decorate finished food on plate with parsley or other piece of food.

Grate
Grind into small pieces by rubbing or scraping on a food grater.

Grease
Grease a baking tray or cookie sheet with butter, margarine, or shortening so the food won't stick to the bottom while baking.

Liquid Ingredients
Fluid ingredients such as water, milk, and eggs.

Liquidize
To beat, blend or boil to change an ingredient from a solid or semi-solid to a liquid.

Melt
Heat ingredients together over a very LOW heat to change from a solid to a liquid.

Mince
Chop up very finely.

Peel
Remove the outer skin or layer of a piece of food with a knife or special peeler.

Saute
Cook in frying pan in a small amount of butter, fat or oil.

Sift
Put any ingredients through a sieve or sifter.

Sieve
A round frame, with wire mesh and a handle, to strain foods.

Simmer
Cook food in a liquid just below boiling on a very LOW heat. Bubbles form slowly and break below the surface.

Stir-fry
Cook in a small amount of hot oil or fat in a frying pan or wok over intense (HIGH) heat with constant, rapid stirring of the ingredients.

Stir
Mix ingredients by moving a spoon or other utensil in a circular motion.

Toss
Mix or toss by turning the ingredients over and over with two forks or two spoons.

Toast
Make crisp and brown by heating.

Whip
Beat vigorously until fluffy or stiff.

Whisk
Combine ingredients together with a wire whisk, using a circular or side-to-side motion.